Also by Ken Crawford:

Yuki

To order, call **1-800-765-6955.**

Visit us at **www.AutumnHousePublishing.com**
for information on other Autumn House® products.

Ossie the Otter

Kenneth C. Crawford

REVIEW AND HERALD® PUBLISHING ASSOCIATION
Since 1861 | www.reviewandherald.com

Published by Autumn House® Publishing, a division of Review and Herald®
Publishing, Hagerstown, MD 21741-1119

Autumn House® titles may be purchased in bulk for educational, business, fund-
raising, or sales promotional use. For information, please e-mail SpecialMarkets
@reviewandherald.com.

Autumn House® Publishing publishes biblically based materials for spiritual, phys-
ical, and mental growth and Christian discipleship.

The author assumes full responsibility for the accuracy of all facts and quotations
as cited in this book.

This book was
Edited by JoAlyce Waugh
Cover designed by Ron Pride
Interior designed by Tina M. Ivany
Cover photo by Jupiterimages
Typeset:Bembo 13/16

PRINTED IN U.S.A.

13 12 11 10 09   5 4 3 2 1

Library of Congress Cataloging-in-Publication Data

Crawford, Ken, 1947-
  Ossie the otter / Ken Crawford.
     p. cm.
  Summary: A five-month-old otter pup tries to survive on its own in the Alaskan
wilderness after being separated from his mother and twin brother.
  1. Otters--Infancy--Alaska--Juvenile fiction. [1. Otters--Fiction. 2. Animals--In-
fancy--Fiction. 3. Alaska--Fiction.] I. Title.
  PZ10.3.C855Os 2009
  [Fic]--dc22

                                          2009023001

ISBN 978-0-8127-0492-1

The sound of solitude,
a dedication

As I recall, it was early on a glorious summer Sunday morning and I was 10 years old. My father stood at the woodstove cooking buckwheat pancakes from a generations-old recipe, and in the background a choir sang hymns on the radio. I stood next to my dad and made a peanut butter and honey sandwich as part of my preparation for a day of wandering alone in the forest. We lived in a tiny village on the edge of a large lake surrounded by wilderness, and my father had taught his children that the forest held no fear, only anticipation.

"Now remember, son," he said in his quiet way, "you have the lake on the south side, Newcastle Creek to the east, the old railway track to the west, and home to the south. You may feel lost at times, but you will be fine as long as you stay within those boundaries. The forest is yours, given by your Creator; go and enjoy it. I will be anxious to hear what you learned today."

I dedicate this book to that memory of my father, for it symbolizes the generations before me who also loved nature. It is truly God's second letter of love.

Contents

Prologue

The short Alaskan summer had passed, and the sharp smell of fall was in the air. Majestic tamarack trees in the lower valleys had turned bright gold, a striking contrast to the deepening red of the higher alpine meadows. On the lower slopes next to a shimmering lake, lofty poplar trees drew sap back to their roots in preparation for a long, cold winter. This part of interior Alaska is a vast wilderness where the presence of man is so rare that seasons pass and generations of animals live and die without witnessing a human footprint or the sound of an axe.

High atop a cliff an adult male eagle perched close to his empty nest. Not long ago, a chick had hatched from an egg in this nest. The eagle glanced toward his mate riding the air currents high above. They would soon leave for the long trip to the southeast coast, and their offspring must practice his flying skills and strengthen his wings. But the male rested, gazing down on the land like a king on his throne. Below the new snowline the endless hillsides had darkened to crimson from the leaves and berries of the high bush cranberries. As he turned his regal head, he caught sight of the rippling movement of brown fur in the distance. Giant grizzlies wandered the slopes, stripping huckleberry bushes of their precious fruit.

At the base of the mountain a great column of steam lifted from Kurupa Lake, a remote, narrow body of water about 10 miles long and one mile wide. The air was colder than the water so the lakes and streams would continue steaming until they froze. The lake water was crystal clear, except for a faint tinge of grey in the upper area where a broad stream flowed into the lake, fed by a massive glacier in the distance.

The northern shoreline of Kurupa Lake sloped gently down to wide gravel beaches where animals came to drink. But along the other side a massive vertical wall scaled the mighty Brooks Mountain Range where the eagles had their nest. Most of these southern slopes were stripped of trees by the spring avalanches that raced down their faces every year. At its western end the lake emptied into a wide, slow moving river. A large pond near the lake also emptied into the river; a family of beavers had created the pond by building a massive dam across a small stream near the lake.

On that particular day the eagle's sharp eyes also took in the aftermath of a recent mud and rock avalanche. Mighty rocks, some larger than houses, lay in random piles along the southern shore of the lake as though an unseen hand had cast them there. Great masses of uprooted trees lay in the water, torn from the mountain by the sudden movement of soggy earth. And beyond the tangle of rocks and fallen trees littering the shoreline, the eagle spied a small creature swimming alone in the clear waters of the lake.

Chapter One

Brand-new Babies!

everal months earlier in late spring Kayla, a North American river otter, had left her mate, Karga, and found a long underwater tunnel below an overhanging bank in the beaver pond. As large flocks of wild geese and swans arrived at the pond and splashed happily about, Kayla worked energetically to enlarge the old tunnel for her needs. She curved the long entrance upward and then dug the den itself above the waterline, just beneath the surface of the ground. Back and forth she went through the tunnel, carrying out mud and material as she worked. Once the den was completed she gathered soft grass and leaves from along the bank and spread them on the floor of the den. Over time they would turn half dry, creating a warm bed and perfuming the air with the musty smell of decaying grass.

Kayla was heavy with pups, and as a first time mother she was anxious about her den. When it was completed to her satisfaction, she curled up in the bed to wait for the moment of birth. Sometimes she awoke to the sound of mice scampering back and forth through their tunnels, grabbing tiny pieces of grass from her bed, then running back to build their own nests. During the night there was a different whimper, and Kayla turned her head to lick the two newborn otter pups lying beside her.

Baby otters are called kits or pups and are helpless at birth. Ossie was the firstborn, measuring five inches from the tip of his little black nose to the base of his tail. As the firstborn otter, he is called the dog pup. His fur was grey and silky soft, much like a pussy willow bud. All otter pups are born toothless and blind and wail like a little baby when they are hungry. Tig the born second; he was smaller, but just as hungry. Kayla spent most of her time curled up around her new pups so they could nuzzle in her soft fur to find their source of milk and so they could stay warm.

Once in a while, when Ossie and Tig were full of milk and sleeping contentedly, Kayla would slip away to find nourishment for herself. She was an expert hunter and could easily catch the fat trout in the pond. Most of the time she would carry her meal to the shore far from the entrance to her den and then eat it quickly while standing partially in the pond. She was always on the alert for any sounds of danger to her little pups. Then with her tummy full and her milk resupplied, she would dive back into the underwater tunnel and climb into the cozy den to be with her pups.

Ossie and Tig were about a month old when their soft blue eyes finally came unglued and they were able to peep out at their mother and their new world. At two months of age the pups were ready to leave the den, but like all otter pups, they were afraid to go into the water. After trying unsuccessfully to coax them into the water, Kayla finally dug a hole up through the roof of the den and lifted her babies up to dry land. She had planned well, and when Ossie and Tig were brought out of the den there was a large, flat grassy area where they could play safely. Whenever a large play area like this is found in the wild, an otter's den may be nearby.

Baby otters grow quickly and love to explore the area outside the den. Soon after Ossie and Tig were old enough to scamper around on the grass, another adult otter appeared. It was their father, Karga. He had stayed away during the birth and while the pups were very young, but he had returned to help raise the two young otters. At first they were afraid of him, but he quickly earned their trust by playing with them in front of the den. He chattered at them and chased them, allowing them to catch and wrestle with him. Soon both pups were following him everywhere. As the pups matured, he took them exploring along the bank of the pond and even ventured into the underbrush. He never stayed with them in the den, but left to sleep alone somewhere beside the lake.

When Ossie and Tig were first brought out to the edge of the pond, they didn't like the water or even the fish and other things that Kayla and Karga brought for them to eat. They only liked pressing their little paws against their mother's soft, warm stomach and drinking the warm, rich milk she provided. But Kayla was patient, and each day she brought the pups something interesting, a partially eaten bit of fish or the remains of a frog, and over time they acquired a taste for the delicious morsels. Soon the brothers were having mock fights, tearing at the pieces and chasing each other around as they played keep-away with the little pieces of flesh. Before long they grew to love the smell of fish or any other small pond creature.

But they were still afraid of water, so Kayla and Karga let the otter pups get used to the cold, clammy feeling slowly. Each parent would let an otter pup climb onto his or her back and then take him swimming around the pond. When the pup became comfortable riding on his parent's back, the adult would slip out from under the pup. At first the otter pups beat the water frantically to stay afloat, and mother or father would slip back under them to support them and make them feel safe. Otters are devoted parents who patiently teach their offspring to swim and how to hunt for their own food.

Soon Ossie and Tig were free-floating and learning to paddle around by themselves. As the summer months went by, the pups became accomplished swimmers and loved being in the water more than playing on land. The pups often played near the den on a rock next to the pond and their favorite activity was pushing each other off into the deep water.

When Ossie and Tig were three months old, they each weighed about six pounds. An average full grown otter weighs between 15 and 25 pounds. In another five or six months it would be possible for the young otter pups to care for themselves, but otter families usually stay together until the birth of a new litter the following year. Young otters generally leave home when they are about 12 to 13 months old.

As the summer progressed, Kayla and Karga took the pups on trips farther and farther from home. In late August, almost five months after the pups were born, Karga left the family to seek out a winter home. Kayla decided to take the pups on an exploratory tour of the lake; it was the pups' first major trip away from the pond where they were born. It was a leisurely yet exciting jaunt for the three of them—exploring streams, chasing trout, and playing on giant mudslides in a vast and exciting wilderness playground. The trip had a purpose, though, since Kayla wanted to teach Ossie and Tig how to fish and how to take care of themselves.

One warm, lingering summer evening, a stiff breeze tossed the waves into whitecaps on the southern shore of the lake. Ossie and Tig played in the water around a great rock pile, wrestling and chasing each other as Kayla watched from a rock on the shore. The three of them had just finished a meal of fish that she had caught, and the pups played with carefree abandon. Thinking that Tig was chasing him, Ossie dived into the deep water off the rocky shoreline, swimming deeper and deeper underwater. Suddenly his world exploded. Huge underwater waves plunged the little otter deeper into the dark, cold depths of the lake. Ossie fought to swim to the surface as wave after wave pushed him relentlessly toward the center of the lake. His lungs bursting, he finally struggled to the surface and gulped in precious air. The little otter had been carried far out into the middle of the lake, and his entire world had changed.

Heavy rains had fallen for several days, softening the soil on the side of the mountain. The wind had started a massive mud and rock avalanche, and huge rocks broke loose and came crashing down the mountain, smashing into the place where Ossie had been with his family. Even as he paddled around on the surface, great waves of muddy water raced across the lake, clawing at him as he was pushed away from the mountain and the danger there. He swam until he was exhausted and then rested, confused and forlorn, on the water's choppy surface. He called for his mother and brother, but there was no answering chatter. He was lost and alone.

Chapter Two

Alone in Paradise

It was a rare and perfect Alaskan day, the air was peaceful and the surface of the lake shimmered like a mirror. Not a ripple broke the stillness of this usually restless water, and the blue sky and the trees on the mountain were perfectly reflected on the surface of the lake. From his perch high above the lake the great eagle watched the southern shoreline for the tiny ripples made by surfacing lake trout. He noticed an ever widening v-shaped ripple not far from the rock-strewn shore. A small creature swam slowly at the surface, a telltale wake trailing behind it. The ripple disappeared when the little animal dived underwater, then reappeared when the creature came back to the surface and continued swimming slowly along the water's edge. The eagle watched intently but didn't move from his perch. If he had been hungry he would have dived from his perch and plucked the small animal from the water.

The ripple was caused by Ossie. Silently and swiftly the baby otter glided through the water so smoothly that he hardly seemed to be moving. Then, holding his short, stubby legs close to his body, the pup dived, twisting his body through the water as does a snake. A sudden burst of bubbles escaped his mouth as he abruptly changed directions with a quick thrust of his webbed hind feet. As his nose broke the surface he took a breath and dived again, cruising at a top speed of six miles per hour. Even though his eyes adjusted easily between underwater and surface viewing, Ossie didn't notice the beauty of his surroundings; he was looking only for his family.

It was strange for the little otter pup to be alone in the large lake, for at only five months of age, Ossie was too young to live by himself. The wilderness of Alaska is a dangerous place for any otter, adult or youngster, to be alone.

Ossie kept swimming until he reached the west end of the lake. There the current flowed faster through marshy flats, and the lake emptied into a wide river outlet. The rushing water wore away the underside of the banks here, and hanging grass draped over the edges. The thick strands waved gracefully underwater, making a good hiding place for fish.

Near the outlet a massive tree lay halfway in the water where it fell, its great trunk partially submerged. Ossie climbed onto the old tree and scampered to the end. Gazing out across the lake he called out in a squeaky, high-pitched whistle, but there was no response. He listened intently, but the only sounds he heard were the soft cackling of geese and the deep croaking of frogs. He couldn't see very far since otters are nearsighted when not in the water, so he used his keen sense of smell and touch.

Ossie lay there on the log in the warm sunshine for a long time. Every few moments he raised his head to sniff the air, his long whiskers twitching and his thick tail flicking back and forth. He was searching for a distinct scent among the odors of wet mud, grass, and decaying leaves. He could smell many things right then, but not his mother or twin brother. Each of them had a certain scent that only the members of their own family knew.

The other animals in the area didn't notice Ossie as he lay quietly on the fallen tree. He had never been away from his family before, so he waited for them to come home to their favorite log. Even after the sun set and bright streams of moonlight sent silver light dancing across the lake, he still lay motionless. Otters are social, fun loving creatures, so it was very unusual for Ossie to stay in one place by himself all day.

Two ravens flew to a nearby tree, hoping to eat the scraps of fish that the otter family usually tossed aside. But Ossie hadn't yet caught a fish by himself, so there were no scraps that day. Disappointed, they flew away to find food somewhere else.

The next morning the pale, golden light of the rising sun cast its beams on the great log, and Ossie awoke. The otter pup thoroughly cleaned and groomed his thick, shiny outer coat. Otters have two coats of fur; the inner coat is made of soft, woolly fur, while the outer coat is long, coarse hair that must be kept straight and clean. This outer coat protects the inner coat from getting wet and must lie flat against the body when the otter swims. Ossie's mother had taught her children how to keep their outer coat clean, and Ossie was careful to follow her example.

Finally he slipped off the log and swam across the river outlet. Scampering out onto the grassy bank, he loped through the tall grass to a large pond not far from the lake. He slipped into the quiet, clear water and dived deep. Large, shadowy trout swam everywhere—fish that could be easily caught—but although Ossie was very hungry, the little otter was on a quest to find his family.

Silently he surfaced and then dived again to explore the undercut of the bank. Turning with a quick twist of his tail, he dived into a hidden underwater hole in the bank. The tunnel twisted and turned before abruptly curving up into the long, narrow entrance of the family den. Ossie climbed out of the watery entrance into the pitch-black darkness of the large, airy den set back in the bank above the waterline. Lingering in the soft, grassy nest was the scent of his family and his mother's milk. He whimpered in anxiety and then fell into a fitful, dream filled sleep.

During the night hunger woke the exhausted pup, but he was reluctant to leave his cozy bed. Eventually his growling tummy drove him back into the pond. By the time he emerged from the den and swam to the surface of the pond, the faint rays of the early morning sun had already turned the sky a vivid pink. A fat blue heron standing on one leg in the shallows squawked in protest when Ossie's furry face suddenly surfaced beside him and disturbed his slumber.

Chapter Three

No Fish

O ssie nosed along the underwater bank, looking for something to eat. Otters have very sensitive whiskers on the nose and elbows which help them find food in murky water. These whiskers even allow them to sense little creatures hidden in the mud. If hungry enough, otters will eat snails, frogs, snakes, turtles, minnows, and even insects.

Ossie was getting weak. It had been several days since he last ate, for his whole focus had been on finding his family. Hunger had driven him from the security of the family den, and although he was still very young, he seemed to understand that he must have food. Instinct led him along the marshy shore for there was always an abundance of water creatures living out their short lives in the backwater of the pond created by the beaver.

He cruised slowly along the muddy shore, nosing out the odd wiggly pond worm or tiny blood sucker, but these were not enough to sustain his active body. He could exist on the frogs and snakes that lived in the pond, but he needed the protein that only fish could provide. Every few moments he came to the surface, gulping air and giving that peculiar little chirping whistle. Otters enjoy hunting, living, and playing together; there are few other creatures that have such a zestful love of life and do things just for the fun of it.

From the edge of the pond the search for food led Ossie closer and closer to the large beaver dam at the end of the pond. Looking up he saw the tiny, webbed feet and plump bodies of baby ducks floating on the surface and the long, spindly legs of the blue heron fishing close to the shore. As he swam along the bottom of the pond, the water grew murky from the mud he was stirring up. All of a sudden he sensed a large trout right in front of him. Otters are incredibly swift, and their favorite food is a nice fat trout. An adult otter can catch a trout up to 30 inches long by sneaking up within 18 inches of the unsuspecting trout, arching their back, and launching their body toward the fish, seizing it as the startled fish tries to swim away.

An adult otter rarely misses, but Ossie was still a pup. With a sudden burst of energy he hurled himself toward the large trout. The big fish streaked away, but Ossie was right on his tail—so close he could almost touch it with his nose. Zigzagging across the pond, the fish tried to elude the hungry otter while searching desperately for shelter.

Otters often try to trap trout in a corner where the fish cannot escape, so Ossie continued to drive the trout along the bank. In a few more months he would have been able to catch this fish quickly and easily, but his mother had still been teaching her pups to hunt when the mudslide occurred. She would catch a fish and bite it just enough to slow it down so her youngsters could chase and catch it. This improved their hunting skills as they learned to survive on their own.

Finally predator and prey reached the deep end of the pond where a grand beaver house stood. The great mud and log house had been built and improved by many generations of beaver families. The twisted sticks jutting randomly into the mud made a natural hiding place for fish. With a flip of his tail the trout dived into the maze, thrusting out his fins to stop quickly. Ossie clawed at the sticks to get at the fish, but it was safe just inches beyond his reach.

He poked at the sticks for awhile, trying to find a way to get through them to his dinner, but he finally ran out of breath and swam to the surface for air. Not only was he disappointed, but he had used a huge amount of energy in the pursuit, further weakening his body. Swimming slowly away, he cruised past the beaver dam toward the shallow end of the pond. If his mother had been there he would have been dining on fresh fish right then.

Instead Ossie explored the shoreline looking for something else to eat. He caught a few more suckers and worms, and then, exhausted, he went back to the den. As he approached the den, he caught the familiar scent of his family and his pace quickened. Whimpering and calling, he swam into the entrance and scampered through the tunnel to the cozy nest. The family den, hidden under the roots of a giant dead cottonwood tree, was a safe haven for Ossie, so he slept peacefully, unaware of the great danger just above him.

Chapter Four

Washed Away

The enormous cottonwood tree had stood alone by the pond for many years and had weathered countless powerful winter storms. Many generations of beaver, muskrats, and otters had lived in this den beneath the safety of its roots. But over the years, water from the pond had weakened its roots, and the giant tree was no longer a mighty stronghold.

Ossie had no sense of how long he slept, but he was awakened by strange movements in and around the den. Tiny wood mice squeaked in terror and ran around wildly inside his dark den. Ossie felt the whole den twisting and rocking; the protective roots of the mighty tree that held the den so securely were beginning to tear from the soil.

He scrambled frantically to the entrance and dived for the safety of deep water. Just then the mighty tree uprooted and crashed to the ground, turning the little den into muddy rubble. The little otter twisted and turned in the water to escape the falling branches as he swam along the muddy bottom of the pond. He had scrambled out of the tunnel entrance just seconds before the massive limbs sliced through the water and drove deep into the soft, oozy bottom. He had just barely avoided being crushed. Finally he surfaced for air in the safety of the deeper water in the center of the pond. When he peered above the choppy surface, it seemed to him that his world had gone mad. A terrible northern storm was whipping the surface of the pond into wild white-caps; but the whitecaps were muddy brown from the silt churned from the bottom of the pond.

Swimming slowly in circles in an attempt to get his bearings, Ossie saw muddy banks exposed along the edge of the pond as the water rushed away. Bewildered little pond creatures were swimming all around him, but he was too frightened to catch and eat any of them. Instinctively he swam back toward his den to survey the scene. The huge cottonwood tree that protected his den had fallen during the tempest and ripped open a gaping hole in the beaver dam. Now precious water rushed through the gap. Ducks, swans, geese, and even the blue heron had left for the safety of the lake. Dazed and confused, he swam closer to where the den had been. Normally Kayla and her pups would have stayed hidden in the den during dangerous storms. But as Ossie swam closer to the old tree, he was suddenly caught in the powerful current of water flooding through the gaping hole in the dam.

Diving again, he tried to swim back to the center of the pond, but the current was too strong. He sensed the danger and instinctively swung hard to the right to cross the current and get to calmer water, but he was too weak. Caught helplessly in the swiftly flowing water, he was sucked downstream toward the jagged opening. The great fallen tree lay across the hole in the dam, its branches creating a tangled, dangerous maze. The limbs seemed to reach out and grab him as he was swept through, and one knotty limb snared him, trapping him underwater.

Ossie struggled to free himself, wriggling his long body until he finally broke loose. Bouncing from limb to limb, he tried to swim through the rest of the muddy maze. But submerged and powerless to fight the current, he was carried rapidly through the gaping hole along with the broken limbs and other debris flooding into the river.

As the raging flood emptied into the river that flowed from the lower end of the lake, Ossie swam helplessly along. The swift current carried him away from the torrent still rushing through the center of the dam to the quietly flowing expanse of the broad river. There the current carried him slowly downstream until he was finally deposited in a calm, sheltered back eddy. Bruised and exhausted, the otter pup floated on his back on the quiet surface, his battered little body sorely in need of rest. He was too tired to climb out onto the shore, so he lay quietly in the gentle back wash of water.

Although the winds were still raging above him, the sheltered water was peaceful, so Ossie allowed his aching body to float lazily in the water under the overhanging grass beside one of the banks for the rest of the stormy night. As morning broke pale and overcast, the young otter swam slowly and painfully along the shore, dining on the banquet of food dislodged from the pond and swept to his little haven.

Chapter five

Double Trouble

As the endless autumn days rolled by, one blurring into another, Ossie spent his time resting and dining on the feast of food washed downriver from the great beaver dam. As he grew stronger, his inner anxiety subsided but still there was no joy. Alone in the wilderness without his family, the beauty and rest in this unfamiliar place was much like a sour note played on a grand piano during a beautiful song. He longed for his family, and this brought on a constant feeling of restlessness.

Autumn was now far advanced, and the snow on the mountaintops had descended into the alpine fields. At times snow fell thick and hard until even the ground at lower altitudes turned white. The

young otter spent his days slumbering in a sheltered grassy depression he had found on the bank
of the wide river and his nights foraging for any
scraps of food he could scavenge in the water
along the banks. He was surviving, but at such a
young age, there was little hope that he would be
able to survive the ravages of an arctic winter.

One calm, sunny afternoon Ossie set out to explore the main river. At first he cautiously hugged
the edge of the river while still allowing the gentle
current to carry him. He kept his head underwater
much of the time watching for minnows or any
other source of food he could spy. The weak sun
warming his back felt good so he let the lazy current carry him farther and farther down the river
alongside the bank.

Suddenly a large shadow appeared above. Startled, and sensing danger, he lifted his head to smell
the air and see if all was well. At that moment
sharp talons stabbed his back and locked into his
flesh. The bird's powerful wings struck both sides
of his body, and Ossie felt himself being lifted
from the water.

Screaming and writhing from shock and pain, he
thrashed about, trying to dive away from the claws
that grasped him tightly. The great wings of an osprey lifted him upward even as he struggled to dive

to safety. The forceful claws tore into his flesh as he twisted desperately one last time and dived back into the water, dragging the mighty osprey with him. The thoroughly drenched bird was now struggling for its own life, and Ossie felt its talons relax as it flapped its wings in a desperate attempt to get out of the water.

Locked together in an embrace of death, osprey and otter suddenly became aware that they had been swept out into the middle of the river. There the forceful current was carrying them rapidly downstream. With a frantic twist of his body and a big gulp of air, Ossie dived again, pulling the soaked bird with him. Finally he broke free and darted away, swimming frantically downstream to get away from the terrible battle.

Wounded and terrified, he immediately had to fight another powerful force. As he was swept downstream, he heard the dull roar of the rapids ahead but he was too weak to resist the current. The raging river hurled the otter pup through a narrow canyon littered with massive rocks. Tumbling through the dirty brown water, Ossie fought to stay close to the surface so he could breathe. The thundering roar of the water drowned out all other sounds as the rushing torrent carried him through its madness until finally the river slowed and he floated into an open area. Blood oozed from his torn back and his legs were too weak to fight the current anymore, so he allowed the river to take him where it would.

The pale, early morning sun peeped over the eastern mountains as the swollen river carried Ossie into an unfamiliar area. Drifting on the gentle surface of a calm backwater he washed up against a large, flat rock beneath an overhanging bank. He climbed out wearily and flopped onto a smooth, algae-covered stone. Overcome with exhaustion, he lost his sense of danger, closed his eyes, and fell into a troubled sleep.

He slept fitfully through the night, his body aching and his dreams full of danger. Finally he awakened when the setting moon sent its bright beams skittering across the water onto the rock where he lay sleeping. His body stiff and sore, he tried in vain to rise and stretch. But, still exhausted, he lay back down and slept again. Late the next afternoon he awakened again, this time from the warmth of the sun shining down on his matted coat. Flies buzzed around the dried blood covering the wounds on his back, so he slipped painfully off the rock into the gentle stream. The cold water soothed his aching muscles and invigorated him. Feeling a little better, he floated along on the gentle current and quickly found hordes of insects and blood suckers washed downstream from the flood. The starving little pup gulped down everything he could reach.

The next few days were warm and sunny, so Ossie explored the area and ate from the plentiful supply of food floating down the river. His normally agile body was still very painful, and he found it difficult to move fast or swim anywhere, so he stayed close to the bank in the quiet water, wary of anything that might harm him.

On the fourth day after being tossed down the rapids he noticed the entrance to a den as he swam slowly along the grassy bank. It was tucked back in the midst of some willows overhanging the bank, and although he caught the musky odor of another animal, his need for shelter was so strong that he dived under the water and cautiously swam into the tunnel. The long tunnel opened into a large den lined with bark stripped from willow trees, the floor covered with dead grass. He sensed that the other animal was there in the den, but he curled up as small as he could in one corner and fell asleep.

Chapter Six

Underwater Antics

Ossie jerked awake when he heard the other animal stirring in the darkness. When it pushed past him toward the entrance, he followed it curiously out into the pond. In the dim evening light he saw that it was a young beaver pup, not much older than himself. Knowing then that it wouldn't hurt him, he swam over cautiously to investigate.

Sage had lived in the great beaver house in the pond; she had been the youngest female in her large family. When the great cottonwood tree fell, she, like Ossie, had been swept through the dam and carried through the river rapids to this place. She had been the first to find the unused den and had made herself at home. Beavers and otters get along very well, and Ossie was glad for the companionship. He followed Sage around the pond for a short while, but she was busy exploring a thick stand of poplar trees in search of something to eat. Finally she found a suitable poplar branch and sat down on the bank, eyeing her newfound friend as she ate. Ossie watched for a while and then lost interest, returned to the tunnel, and fell asleep again.

Beavers are nocturnal, which means that they usually sleep during the day and are most active at night. So when Sage returned to the den at dawn, Ossie had slept and was ready to begin his day.

The little otter spent the following days exploring along the shore and finding more blood suckers and frogs to eat. One cold, blustery day as Ossie was investigating the area, he dived to the bottom to feel his way through the gentle undercurrent along cuts in the bank. Farther and farther he swam downstream until the icy water suddenly turned warm. Surfacing, he looked around and found that there was a small side stream flowing into the river. Far upstream hot mineral water boiled out of the ground and large columns of steam rose, twisting and curling, in the cold air. Where the warm waters of the hot spring joined the river, the water flowed into a natural rock enclosure and filtered through the rocks into the stream.

Ossie climbed painfully over the rocks and paddled around in the warm mineral water of the little pond. The warm water was so soothing to his wounds that he lingered in the rock enclosure until sunset. Then, as he slipped over the edge back into the river, he spotted a large school of trout milling around the rock enclosure. The trout gathered here to wait for insects and other food to filter through the rocks into the river. With a flip of his tail, Ossie dived to chase one of them, but he still didn't have the strength or speed to catch the fat fish.

Disappointed, he swam slowly back to his den and crept in through the entrance. Sage had slept the day away, and as Ossie nosed her, she awakened and grunted at him. She seemed glad that he had returned, but before long she left the cave to spend the night finding food for her own needs. This quickly became a daily routine. Ossie would awaken each morning to the sound of Sage entering the den, and she would usually nuzzle him before she lay down. Sometimes if he awakened early he would wait for her to come in before leaving the den. The two little orphans had formed an unlikely but close friendship.

Ossie spent most of his days lingering around the hot spring, feeding along the banks, and trying his best to catch the swift trout that hung around the rock enclosure. He seemed to sense that the warm mineral water helped to heal his wounds, but although the water was healing the wounds of his flesh, it could not reach the inner longings of his heart. He missed his mother and his brother; he missed the companionship of family. Instinctively he knew he must begin his journey again, yet the same inner instinct told him that he must wait until he was stronger.

The autumn days were getting colder, though, and the days increasingly shorter. The weakening sun had lost much of its warmth and rose lower on the southern horizon each passing day. The summer snowfield and glacier meltwater feeding the lake slowed, and the water level in the river began to drop. Fresh snow brought on by the chill of the oncoming winter covered the dirty brown surfaces of the mountains and glaciers like a clean, white blanket.

Swan families had been practicing their formation flights day after day, and their trumpeting calls of encouragement to the young swans echoed from the hills. Then one day they left. It was as if the Creator had given some hidden signal to all the swans at once. In a noisy fanfare of loud calls and flurrying wings, they lifted off from the river and flew away to some destination they alone knew. Only a few days later, ducks began arriving from the northern arctic tundra. The river, so recently the summer home to an endless number of exotic birds, became the resting place for thousands more that were migrating south. Curlew sandpipers and golden plovers flocked to the river, and bar-tailed godwits stopped for a final rest before their nonstop, 7,500-mile trip from the arctic to the shores of New Zealand.

One morning when Ossie emerged from the den, Sage was busy preparing an underwater supply of food for when the river froze. The industrious beaver had dragged poplar branches into the water and was pushing them into the mud at the bottom. Next summer she would try to extend a dam out from the bank to back up the slow-moving water.

Ossie was feeling much better by now and had awakened in a playful mood, so he dived into the shallow water and swam underwater to Sage. Otters love to wrestle, so Ossie thought he would tussle with Sage as he used to do with his brother, Tig. Without warning, Ossie grabbed Sage's broad tail with his front feet and hung on. Poor Sage was so startled that she jumped forward to dive for safety and tried to slap her tail on the water at the same time. But when she lifted her powerful tail, Ossie flew through the air over her head and splashed into the water right in front of her just as she dived under. Sage ran headlong into him, of course, and knocked the wind out of him. In her haste the frightened little beaver never stopped to see who her assailant was; she just swam with all her might to the deepest part of the river. When Ossie finally caught his breath, he looked across the river only to see Sage glaring at him as if to say, "What kind of dumb trick was that? You almost scared me out of my skin!"

Chapter Seven

The Ill-tempered
Moose in the Pantry

Instinct told Ossie that he could stay here in the river during the winter. The warm water would run freely, which meant that the fish would also remain in the river for the winter. The den he shared with Sage was cozy, and her companionship would make the cold months bearable. However, something within him yearned to return to his home on the lake where he had been born. He couldn't quite shake that inner longing for the companionship of family, and part of him dreaded spending the winter without them. Karga, his father, would probably return to the den to spend the winter with his family, and Ossie wanted to be back at the lake when he arrived.

One cold, snowy fall day Ossie explored his watery home a little farther out from shore than usual. He was tired of living on the tiny creatures he found here and there and longed for a fat, tasty trout. Early in the evening he swam along the rocky bottom to the center of the river and then around the banks of the far shore. There in the dim light filtering through the water, he sensed rather than saw another creature swimming underwater. It was a merganser, a diving duck, searching for fish. Ossie watched hungrily as the expert fisher snatched a fat trout and glided back to the surface. On impulse, Ossie dashed after it and rammed the duck's fat belly with his snout just as it reached the surface. Surprised, the merganser shot out of the water, losing its grip on the trout. Ossie seized the fish and plunged deep into the river. Swimming as fast as he could, he made his way along the bank to a flat rock and then surfaced. With some difficulty he hauled out his stolen dinner and began tearing it apart with relish. The merganser let out a disgruntled squawk and went back to fishing for her brood.

Soon the winter ice grew thick along the edges of the river, and the haunting call of the migrating Canada geese echoed across the water. The geese arrived to rest just after the swans left, and sometimes their silhouettes could be seen in the moonlight as they floated safely on the water away from the shoreline. Every morning the merganser family took to the air, lifting off from the river to make long treks around the mountain range in order to strengthen the wings of their young.

Loons took flight for unknown places in the south, yet Ossie still lingered to soak in the mineral pool and regain his strength. Each day he spent several hours immersed in the warm water, and though the air was crisp and brittle with the first gusts of winter cold, he felt his body healing. In order to survive the winter, however, he needed to be strong enough to catch fish. Every day he slipped over the rock enclosure and tried to catch some of the elusive trout prowling around the warm water outlet. One day, in hot pursuit of one of the plump fish, he veered to one side just in time and caught it. Every day after that he managed to catch at least one fish—now he could survive the winter on his own.

Sage was quite content with her new home and stayed busy putting up a store of food for the winter by cutting down several large poplar trees. The fallen trees attracted the attention of a huge bull moose who decided to take up residence in Sage's wilderness pantry. It was mating season, and the bull spent a lot of time thrashing around in the branches of the fallen trees to clean and strengthen his enormous antlers in preparation for battle.

At night his mournful calls echoed across the valley, and his habit of tromping heavily above the den made both Sage and Ossie nervous. The big moose seemed to have a short temper, and sometimes both otter and beaver watched uneasily from the safety of the water as the moose dismantled large trees and broke them into pieces. This mock fighting helped the bull judge the strength and length of his horns and gave him practice for upcoming battles for a female.

As the days went by, Sage grew increasingly nervous because the moose had staked out his territory right in the center of her poplar grove. One evening she and Ossie were both out on the river watching their seemingly crazed neighbor in one of his rampages. Ossie swam cautiously along the river's edge, but Sage, anxious to get to work, crept out of the water and made her way to the stand of trees where she had been working. The moose was still stomping around the grove, and she didn't want to set off one of his ill-tempered outbursts.

Skirting the edge of the clearing to stay away from the moose, she tiptoed to a poplar tree that she had been working on for several nights, braced herself with her strong, flat tail, and began gnawing at its base. She had worked her way through most of the trunk during the nights when the moose was gone, and the tree was nearly ready to topple. Her plan was to fell the tree into the water and then use it to hold other branches underwater so she would have food during the winter. Amazingly, beavers have the ability to sense which way a tree will fall and adjust the direction of the fall with their teeth.

As Ossie swam close to the shore to watch, he noticed that Sage's presence seemed to make the bull angry. She didn't seem to notice, though, and finished her task of chewing through the tree's trunk. When the mighty tree cracked and groaned, the angry bull thought he heard a rival bull moose entering his territory. In his rage the moose attacked the little beaver as the tree began tilting toward the water.

Sage had backed away from the tree to watch it fall and was standing in the open when the moose attacked. The moose reared up on his hind legs and brought his hooves smashing down, but Sage darted away just in time. He charged again, his ears flat against his head, the hair on the back of his neck standing straight up. Just as it seemed there was no escaping his fury, the poplar tree came crashing down. The branches of the falling tree caught the bull's massive antlers and flung him to the ground, twisting his neck to one side and pinning him to the floor of the clearing.

The confused moose lay there for a moment and then began flailing around frantically in an attempt to get out from under the tree. Sage flew past the moose to the safety of the river and slapped her tail loudly against the water as she dived under. The bull finally freed himself from the tangled branches and proceeded to vent his rage on the tree. He quickly stripped the limbs with his antlers and then stomped the branches into the soft ground as he searched for the creature that had caused him so much misery.

He reared again and slammed the ground with his front hooves, but his feet broke through into Sage and Ossie's den. His legs sank down to his knees into the ground, which made him even angrier. In just a few seconds the powerful moose destroyed their home as he tried to get out of the hole he had made in the ground. Finally he worked himself loose and stomped off in a sullen rage.

Chapter Eight

A Narrow Escape

From the safety of deep water, Ossie had watched the moose's temper tantrum with fascination, and for the rest of the night he and Sage stayed in the water away from their ruined den. Late the next morning Sage returned to the den to survey the damages. Finding it completely destroyed, she began working on another den not far away. A sense of urgency drove her efforts as she dug her new tunnel; time was short. But Ossie swam back to the warm mineral pool to catch trout and ponder his future.

Late in the day the cold autumn wind blew dark gray clouds over the sun—another storm was descending on the river. The Canada geese gathered their young and lifted off into the blustery winds, their voices echoing across the valley as they honked a final goodbye to their wilderness resting place. Forming a ragged V-formation, they headed south on the swift air currents. Ossie watched them leave and sensed that winter was coming soon; but now he had no home to protect him from the elements.

He stayed close to the hot springs pool until he caught another fat trout and carried it to a large, flat rock. Still afraid to venture out of the water, he ate his dinner in the river. Big, fluffy snowflakes began to fall, swirling and tumbling in the wind. Soon the ground was covered with a white snowy blanket. Ossie had never seen snow before, so he swam slowly upstream and then backtracked to his warm pool. He didn't want to leave this familiar place, but the call of home was so strong that he finally swam upstream past the den he had shared with Sage. As he followed the curve of the river, he tested the water for familiar scents, but found nothing. Even the ground was white and strange. He didn't remember this part of the river since he had been too injured the day he was swept through the rapids, but instinct urged him ever onward.

Darkness fell, but he kept swimming until the current became too strong. Now the river seemed to have turned against him, and although his little body was no match for the rushing water of the rapids, he fought the current until he was exhausted. Finding a grassy bank, the weary little otter climbed out of the water to rest. He nosed around in the snow until he found a hollow underneath a low hanging alder bush, crawled under it, and fell asleep.

When daylight finally came, the world looked pale, cold, and unfriendly. The sun shone weakly through the still swirling snow as Ossie awakened and stretched slowly. He lay still for a long time, gazing at the water crashing over the rocks. He seemed to understand that he could not swim against its relentless power again, so he stayed where he was, waiting and resting.

Finally he decided to continue his journey, so he left his resting place and scampered along the steep, snow covered bank. He followed it as best as he could, trying to stay within earshot of the roaring water. Loping along on his short, stubby legs, he traveled for several hours before he came to a cottonwood grove and descended a steep hill to a gravel bar in the river. Here the flood had left a series of pools where tiny minnows darted around in the clear water. He scurried after them and caught enough to stop the growling of his empty stomach. He didn't linger long, though, for he was vulnerable to predators when he wasn't in the water.

The setting sun, white behind the distant southern mountains, cast faint shafts of light ahead of the little otter as he continued to run along the riverbank. Exhausted at last, he crawled under the root of a large tree and lay gazing out at this strange, snowy world. Eventually he closed his eyes and slept.

Some time later he was awakened by the sound of an animal gnawing on something. Thinking of his friend, Sage, he listened quietly. Out of the corner of his eye, he caught sight of a large rabbit tearing bark from the roots of the tree under which he was hiding. The rabbit's coat was a mottled brown and white since it was changing colors from summer brown to winter white. The rabbit seemed aware of Ossie's presence, but paid little attention to him. But it did act nervous, and every few minutes, it jerked upright and thumped its foot on the ground.

Suddenly Ossie smelled a strange, musty odor that grew stronger and stronger. The rabbit noticed it too and began thumping its back feet in panic. Out of the darkness, a large wolverine appeared. Wolverines are a larger cousin of otters, but are mean animals that will kill and eat just about anything. Even grizzly bears avoid adult wolverines. This particular wolverine had been following the rabbit's trail with his keen sense of smell, and now he quickly closed in on his prey.

Not wanting to be the wolverine's midnight snack, the rabbit bounded out from under the roots of the tree and dashed away with the wolverine in hot pursuit. Rabbits can outrun most predators, but only for a short period of time. The wolverine chased the rabbit for a while and then lost interest. He ambled back toward the tree and then stopped abruptly to sniff the ground. Scurrying back to the tree with his nose to the ground, he followed Ossie's trail back to the tree.

Ossie had held perfectly still until then, hoping that he had not been discovered, but when he caught the strong odor of the wolverine again, he knew he was in danger. The wolverine was still hungry and intended to make Ossie his next meal. As the wolverine came closer, Ossie darted out from under the tree and ran for his life. Wolverines have poor eyesight, but this one spotted the fleeing otter and raced after him.

Glancing back over his shoulder, Ossie saw the wolverine's white teeth gleaming as it pursued him. The wolverine was big and strong and much faster than the otter pup, and it was quickly closing the gap between them. Ossie dodged trees and ducked under low bushes as he ran, but the wolverine was determined to catch this meal. Finally out of breath and unable to keep up the mad dash any longer, Ossie spotted a long, steep grassy hill covered with a light dusting of snow just ahead. In desperation he threw himself over the edge of the hill and tobogganed down on his belly, his paws tucked up to make him slide faster. The wolverine scrambled down after him, but couldn't keep up as Ossie streaked down the hill.

Ossie had no idea where the hill would end because the snow was spraying into his eyes as he slid. He just knew that he must escape. The wolverine plowed after him, following the billowing snow trail. He lost sight of Ossie for an instant, but continued scrambling down the steep incline after the fleeing otter.

At the bottom of the hill was a large, muddy backwater created by the flood. Thin ice had formed along the edge and extended out several feet over the water. Ossie was going so fast when he reached the bottom of the hill that he whooshed across the ice and plunged into the cold water. The wolverine dashed across the ice, but his heavier body broke through and he thrashed around, searching wildly for his prey. He was an excellent swimmer and finally broke through the rest of the ice to the place where Ossie had disappeared. He swam around in circles, waiting for his prey to surface.

But Ossie knew better than to come up right away. He swam underwater, feeling his way along the bottom, until his lungs were ready to burst. At a bank where the water was moving and there was no shore ice, he cautiously lifted his mouth to the surface to take a breath and dived again. Slowing his heartbeat, he sank to the bottom and waited.

Wet and angry, the wolverine splashed around in the river for a long time before he finally climbed back up onto the ice and ran off in search of other prey.

Chapter Nine

Home at Last

Ossie lingered in the water as long as he could and then scrambled out on the far side of the river. For most the day, the frightened little otter ran cautiously along the opposite edge of the river and away from danger. Finally he slipped back into the water and continued swimming upstream. The terrain had changed during his flight from the wolverine, and the land had become rough and hilly. Although the river was swifter here, it was easier to swim against the current than to run on land. When darkness fell he climbed out of the water and found a hollow spot in the grass where he could curl up in a ball and sleep.

Before dawn broke, he dived back into the water and continued his long, strenuous journey. After a while the river narrowed and became too swift for him to continue swimming upstream any longer. It had been two days since he had found anything to eat, and his growling tummy sent him again to the river's edge. Exhausted, and remembering the wild ride he'd taken through these rapids, he scouted carefully along the shore.

Not far from the rapids was a quiet pool where the water swirled slowly. Ossie sensed that there were trout in this pool, so he dived in. In fact, there were several fat trout awaiting him, so he caught one, ate it with relish, and then slid back to the riverbank. Experience had taught him to stay out of the rushing water until he was past the rapids, and instinct told him which direction to travel to get home.

The wind finally died down, and only a few flakes of snow drifted lazily in the frigid air. High overhead the moon cast strange shadows across the white, snowy ground. Ossie ran parallel to the roar of the rapids, trying to stay as close as he could to the water. He didn't care that he was leaving a crooked trail in the snow that any predator could follow, but continued his journey home.

Hour after hour he ran, even slithering across the muddy ground at times. Once he fell into a strange grassy bog called a muskeg and only got out by half swimming and half running. On and on he ran through the night until the grey dawn sent icy beams of light down through the nearly barren trees. He couldn't find a place to hide and rest, so he pressed on until he could finally see the glimmer of the river in the distance.

Otters are more at home in the water than on land. They tend to run with a hump in their backs, and they tire quickly because of their short legs. Ossie was completely worn out, but driven by fear of the unknown he thought only of reaching the safety and comfort of calm water. The sun was shining weakly above him by the time he finally dived into the river a safe distance beyond the rapids.

Floating on the soft, gentle cushion of water, Ossie let his weary body relax. He wasn't safe yet, but he was relieved to be back in the water. Once again hunger urged him to search for food, but there were no fish to be found. He explored the edge of the river and ate whatever little creatures he could find. As he rambled about, he found shelter under a low overhanging rock, so he crawled under it and slept for the rest of the day.

The vivid colors of a beautiful Alaskan sunset were lingering on the horizon when he finally ventured out from under his rock and swam along the shore toward the lake. Soon he came to the mouth of the stream that emptied into the river from the beaver pond, and he followed it all the way to where it had emptied through the gaping hole in the beaver dam.

The mighty poplar tree still lay across the jagged opening, the branches above water waving in the breeze. Using the fallen tree as a solid anchor, the beaver family had built a new, stronger dam. This new dam had raised the water level in the pond higher than it had been originally, but Ossie didn't care, he was just glad to see his old home again.

Scampering across the dam, he slid into the pond. It felt wonderful to be back in his home pond! He happily explored the shoreline and found an old, abandoned muskrat den along the bank. Exhausted from his long trip, he crawled in, curled up, and fell into a deep sleep, even though the smell of the muskrats was still quite strong.

The next morning a sheet of ice had formed at the edge of the pond. Each morning the sheet of ice extended a little farther out from the banks, shrinking the area of open water in the center. Ossie didn't mind, but continued to rest and fish in the depths of the pond. He was older, stronger, and wiser than when he had been swept away earlier in the fall. He was content to spend the winter here,

but this showed his inexperience since he didn't re-
alize that he wouldn't be able to open a hole in the
ice to get in and out of the water. Otters usually
gather by a fast running stream during the winter
so they have open water in which to catch fish.
Ossie stayed there, resting and fishing, for several
more days, but he was in great danger. The temper-
ature continued to drop, and the bitter cold of winter would soon freeze the pond shut like a trap. As
winter descended on the pond the voices of the
marsh became silent, and the frogs buried themselves in mud to sleep away the winter.

One chilly day Ossie had an urge to explore the
old log where his family had spent so much of
their time. Emerging from the muskrat den, he
slipped and slithered across the shore ice and scurried across the stretch of land separating the pond
from the lake. Sliding across the final stretch of
shore ice, he dived into the cold, clear water of
the lake and swam to the place where the dead
tree's massive trunk still jutted out into the water.
He scampered out to the end of the tree and lay
down. The sun's pale warmth caressed his wet fur,
and he dozed off.

When he awoke, the sky was a deep, but pale,
crimson color. Beyond the mountains to the south-
west, the setting sun cast soft rays of light across the

calm lake. It was a beautiful sight, but it brought back strong memories of the first day he had come here alone. His little heart was overcome with a great longing for his family and for companionship. He had been surviving on his own for nearly two months now. As he lay there on the end of the log, gazing out across the still waters, he suddenly raised his head and stared at something in the lake with growing interest. A small v-shaped ripple was moving toward him from the mouth of the lake, skirting the ice along the shore. The ripple disappeared for a moment and appeared again a little closer. Ossie watched intently as the creature causing the ripple slowly made its way closer and closer.

All of a sudden Ossie leaped off the old log, raced across the ice, and plunged into the chilly water. Rather than swimming away to escape the creature coming toward him, he dived deep and swam directly toward it. Looking up at it from below, he could clearly see the form above him. The creature dived suddenly and came straight for him. But instead of darting away, Ossie swam right to it. When they met, they locked their front legs and swirled around under the water together in a tight spiral. Their exuberant dance sent water foaming in ever widening circles when they finally broke the surface.

The other creature was a large, handsome adult otter. It was Karga, his father, who had come home to spend the winter with his family. Ossie was safe, and his long, dangerous journey was over.

The last faint rays of the sun shone on the lake as two v-shaped ripples moved slowly along the shore. Two otters, father and son, made their way eastward along the shoreline toward the head of the lake in search of the rest of their little family, hoping for a grand reunion with mother and twin.

Meet Four Amazing Adventist Girls

You'll be swept back in time with these true stories about six generations of Adventist gir[ls] The exciting series weaves through changi[ng] times, beginning with Ann, born in 1833, and ending with Erin, who is a teenager today. Read *Hannah's Girls* because every girl has a special story, a rich history, and a great heri[tage] as a daughter of God.

The first four books of a six-book series

Ann (1833-1897)
0-8280-1951-4

Marilla (1851-1916)
0-8280-1952-1

Grace (1890-1973)
0-8280-1953-8

Ruthie (1931-)
0-8280-1954-5

Paperback.

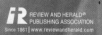